MW01285037

Jimmy and the Big Jurtle

Jim Haskin

authorHOUSE®

AuthorHouse™
1663 Liberty Drive
Bloomington, IN 47403
www.authorhouse.com
Phone: 1-800-839-8640

First published by AuthorHouse 7/20/2009

ISBN: 978-1-4389-9762-9 (e)
ISBN: 978-1-4389-9760-5 (sc)
ISBN: 978-1-4389-9761-2 (hc)

Printed in the United States of America
Bloomington, Indiana

This book is printed on acid-free paper.

CHAPTER ONE

June 1ˢᵗ, 1943

Jimmy was running late, he might miss the school bus. Yesterday the bus driver warned him he wasn't going to wait the next time he was late for the bus. Union Lake School was a mile away, a long walk for an almost ten-year-old boy. Jimmy was racing full speed with his head down; he raised his eyes to check on his progress. There were three more in line to board the bus, he might make it. Out of breath, with beads of sweat on his forehead, he skidded to a halt on the loose gravel as he reached for the handle to board the bus. The bus driver had his hand on the lever that closed the door. "Good work Jimmy, you just made it."

His friend Roger had saved him a seat, and he was laughing as Jimmy sat down.

"What takes you so long in the morning?"

Before Jimmy could catch his breath to answer the question, Roger started to laugh again, saying, "Where's your lunch? Did you forget your lunch?"

Jimmy shook his head; he had forgotten his lunch. What made it worse, it was Friday. On Friday his mother made his favorite sandwich, tuna fish. He sighed, thinking this wasn't going to be a good day. No lunch and he hadn't read the last two chapters of *Little House on the Prairie*. He hoped the teacher wouldn't call on him. "My sister Iris hogged the bathroom. Can I have half of your sandwich if my mother doesn't bring my lunch?"

"You can have half of my sandwich, but you don't like cheese."

"Thank you for sharing. My mother says that beggars can't be picky eaters." Jimmy smiled and slapped Roger on the shoulder. "Can you believe it? School will be out next week and fishing season opens the following Thursday. You're already ten, and I'll be ten in three weeks. We can take the boat out on our own." Last summer without the boat, Jimmy and Roger would wade in the water to a depth that was chest high and use their long bamboo poles to reach the edge of the drop-off. The small pan fish they caught swam on or near the drop-off where the weeds grew. Frequently their lines would get tangled there and the little bluegills would steal their worms. Roger wasn't five feet tall, and he complained that Jimmy always caught more fish because he was taller and could go farther out in the water. Roger gave Jimmy a serious look. "I bet my brother Ron a quarter we catch twenty-five fish on opening day." Ron was two years older and last year he took Roger and Jimmy fishing on opening day so they could use the boat.

Jimmy thought that a quarter was a big bet for Roger, as some weeks he didn't make a quarter. "That's a lot of fish; and they're hard to catch. We've never caught that many, and you might lose a quarter."

"We're older now, and this year we can use the boat. A friend gave my father a net and we can catch minnows off the dock. We can fish with minnows and worms. That's what Mr. Robinson does, and he always catches fish." Mr. Robinson was the best fisherman on Union Lake, and he caught big pike and bass. He threw back the little rock bass, sunfish, perch and blue gills that Jimmy and Roger caught.

The bus arrived at school, with only nine more days to go before summer break. It was hard to go to school when the sun was shining, and you wanted to go fishing.

Jimmy and Roger were the only ten-year-old boys in their immediate neighborhood. They lived a block apart and had been inseparable since Roger's family moved to Union Lake when he was in the third grade. Roger had two older sisters, a brother Ron who was two years older, and his brother Don was a year younger. The four boys played baseball and football together and if someone needed help they would work together. The other kids called Jimmy and Roger Mutt and Jeff. Jimmy was the biggest kid in the class and Roger was the smallest. Jimmy's sister Iris was three years older and his brother Hugh was five years his senior. Jimmy's family was tall, Hugh was fourteen and six foot-three inches tall, the same height as his dad, and Jimmy was the tallest boy in the school. Jimmy's father said more was expected from the bigger kids and he would have to act his height and not his age.

Jimmy's mother brought his lunch; it would have been better to go hungry. His mother and teacher were discussing his schoolwork, and that was always bad news. Jimmy did just enough to get by; he wasn't considered a good student. After lunch his eyes turned to the window and the bright sunshine. He imagined it was the opening day of fishing season. He could sense the gentle rocking of the boat and in his mind he could picture the red and white bobber bouncing on top of the water. Suddenly the bobber disappeared under the water as the fish took the bait. He pulled up, the tip of the bamboo pole was severely bent; it was a big fish, maybe a bass? The teacher called his name, but Jimmy didn't answer, he was busy catching the fish. "Wake up, Jimmy, and pay attention. I asked you a question about *Little House on the Prairie.*"

The teacher's question startled him and he stammered, "I-I-I-I didn't feel well last night; I went to bed early."

"No more poor excuses. You can stay after school and do your homework. Walking home will be good for you. Not everyone will be promoted to the fifth grade. Those who can't keep up will repeat the fourth grade."

Mary and Sally were laughing. Mary whispered to Sally, "Jimmy's already the biggest kid in the class. He'll really be big for a fourth grader."

Sally snickered at Jimmy, saying, "You're not smart enough to stay out of trouble."

Jimmy scowled. Sally didn't have that long pigtail anymore. In the third grade Jimmy got spanked for putting Sally's pigtail in the inkwell. But the schoolwork wasn't that hard. He would work harder and pass the fourth grade.

On his walk home Jimmy was planning his last days of school. "I'll do my homework first thing and have my sister Iris check it." Iris was smart and got good grades. He smiled, thinking, "I'm a good writer, and I'll do well on my book report." It was approaching five o'clock when Jimmy started up the driveway. His dog King ran to greet him. The dog jumped on Jimmy and wouldn't stop until the boy put his books down and hugged the dog. King was part collie, part husky and part of another breed that gave him his jet-black coat. An elderly woman who was unable to care for the dog gave him to Jimmy last year. Jimmy and King bonded quickly, and everywhere Jimmy went, King was at his heels. King was five years old and well trained. He was car smart and didn't chase cars or run on Union Lake Road when Jimmy went to the grocery store. The dog loved to play in the water, and liked being in the boat. He would rest under the seat at Jimmy's feet. Jimmy couldn't imagine life without King.

CHAPTER TWO

Union Lake

Union Lake Village was located in Oakland County, Michigan. Oakland County was known for its many lakes, and Union Lake was one of its best. The lake had depths from very shallow on the eastern shore to a depth of 110 feet at the center of the lake. A drop-off was dangerously close to most of the shoreline where a swimmer could go from water neck high to well over their head in one stride. Swimmers who feared they were drowning in deep water could be rescued by someone who would reach out and pull the swimmer to safety three or four feet from where they were in trouble. There were areas on the south shore where a swimmer could dive off the bank into five feet of water. Because of the lake's depth, cool water, steep drop-offs, and under water caves, many fish and turtles grew to extraordinary sizes. The many cold water springs that fed the lake produced an overflow that was controlled by a small dam where water was released into a stream that ran to Long Lake. Unlike many of the surrounding lakes, Union Lake didn't lose water during the summer droughts.

The residents of Oakland County identified with the lake they lived on or near. Jimmy and Roger were from Union Lake, a schoolmate was from Round Lake, there were twin sisters from Lower Middle Straits Lake, and the kids from Westacres were from Middle Straits Lake. Most of their classmates at Union Lake School were from one lake or another. The lakes had access through privilege lots that were owned by the residents who lived near the lake, but not on the lake. Their ownership was recorded in their property deed and access to the privilege lots was limited to property owners. Union Lake Village was located between three lakes, Cooley Lake to the Northwest, Long Lake to Southwest, and Union Lake to the Southeast.

Long lake and Cooley Lake were shallow lakes half the size of Union Lake. They were choked with weeds and filling up with sediment and muck. Some residents living on Long Lake were unable to use the lake during the July and August dry season when the receding water level turned the two bays into muddy goo. It was a strange sight to see docks with no water beneath them and boats sitting on the mud with no access to the usable part of the lake. There was talk of pumping out Long Lake to remove the sediment. Most of the homes on the three lakes were summer cottages that were owned by people from Detroit or Highland Park. The population of Union Lake more than doubled in the summer months when the cottages were occupied.

Union Lake Village had two small grocery stores and a gas station. The Great War (World War II) had changed life at Union Lake. The adults were busy working in the defense factories in nearby Pontiac and had little time for fishing and boating. Everything Jimmy's family needed was rationed, from gasoline and tires, to food and sugar. His mother needed coupons to buy the rationed items, and the school boards were responsible for issuing the coupons. Jimmy's mother picked her coupons up once a month at Union Lake School. If a family ran out of coupons for sugar toward the end of the month, they had to wait until the next month before they could purchase more. The federal government had imposed a thirty-five-mile-an-hour speed limit on all roads to conserve gasoline. The reduced speed limit added thirty minutes to Jimmy's father's commute time to Detroit. His father carpooled with four other men to conserve gasoline and wear and tear on their tires and cars. The speed limit and gasoline rationing also discouraged the people from Detroit who owned cottages on the lakes from taking frequent trips. Many families didn't use their cottages until the Fourth of July holiday.

Most of the boys and some of the girls graduating from high school joined the Army or Navy. Two boys from Cedar Island Lake, a small community two miles from Union Lake, had been killed fighting in North Africa. It seemed like every home and store had an American flag prominently displayed. The war began when Jimmy was eight, and he had few memories of life before the war.

Jimmy and Roger had a summer friend, Jerry, who was a year older and lived in Detroit. Jerry's family had a cottage on Union Lake next to the privilege lot. The privilege lot was on the south end of a small bay where the boys would fish and swim. Across the bay was the fishing site. The site was owned and managed by the State of Michigan. Unlike the local privilege lots, the place offered public access to Union Lake and fishermen used the site to launch their boats.

Jimmy and his friends would row for hours exploring Union Lake, and dropping the anchor to see how deep the water was. They used three fifty-foot ropes to reach the bottom in the middle of the lake. Just last summer they saw a giant Leatherback Turtle swimming on the bottom near the drop-off. Union lake had many Leatherback Turtles and they were good-sized, but this one looked as big as a wash tub. You could spot the Leatherback Turtles by their pointed noses when they came up for air. The Leatherbacks were powerful swimmers with large front and rear flippers and a strong bite. They were fast swimmers and their flipper-like legs were equipped with sharp claws.

Last summer Jimmy caught a seven-inch Leatherback Turtle on his fishing pole. He tried to remove the hook but the turtle bit him on his index finger causing the finger to bleed. His brother donned leather gloves and removed the hook. They released the turtle back into the lake. Jimmy mentioned the incident to Mr. Marohn, and he said the big turtles had been there since he was a small boy. "In

Union Lake, everything grows bigger in the cooler water, and most people that use the lake have never seen a big Leatherback Turtle up close or caught one of those large Northern Pikes. Years ago my uncle caught a Northern Pike that was forty-two inches long. He said he was fishing in eighty feet of water. I don't know if anybody keeps records on who has caught the biggest fish, but that was the biggest pike I've ever seen. A big Northern Pike speared in the winter or caught in the summer is three feet or smaller."

Union Lake was a wonderful place to grow up. Each resident knew everyone else, and there was always something to do. In the summer, one could go swimming, play baseball and go fishing and in the winter, sledding, ice-skating and hockey were common pastimes. Union Lake froze over in the winter, and the fishermen used the fishing site to drive their cars on the lake. They cut holes in the ice and either fished for or speared Northern Pike and large bass. Some of the pikes were three feet long, the biggest fish Jimmy had ever seen. Some fishermen had ice shanties with wood-burning stoves to stay warm while they fished. It was quite a sight to see four or five cars parked on the lake and smoke rising from the chimneys of the ice shanties on a clear sunny day. Mr. Robinson had an ice shanty, and he would spear bass and pike in the winter. He would dangle an artificial lure three to four feet under water, and spear the fish as it struck the lure. The fish were set on the ice outside the shanty and Roger and Jimmy would marvel at their size.

Jimmy was bigger and stronger than he was last summer. He had earned $4.75 raking lawns and doing yard work for the older people that lived in the neighborhood. Being ten made a difference, and this summer he could caddy at the golf course, mow lawns and clean garages.

CHAPTER THREE

School's Out

School was out, and Jimmy and Roger were promoted to the fifth grade. Jimmy breathed a sigh of relief; it was the second time in three years the teacher threatened to hold him back. Jimmy and his brother Hugh were helping their father dig a new drainage field for the septic tank. They were completing the sixth long trench across the yard. The sandy soil made the digging easier then expected, and they were almost finished by lunch. After lunch, Roger came over; it was time to get ready for the opening day of fishing season. There was less than ten feet of digging left, and Jimmy's brother and a friend said they would finish the task.

Jimmy and Roger were serious fishermen, and it was time to check the contents of the tackle box. Needed were a package of mixed hooks and a package of sinkers. The spool of line was depleted and they needed new bobbers. If they caught twenty-five fish, another fish stringer would be handy, as a stringer held fifteen fish. If there were any money left, they would buy a fish scaler. Cleaning twenty-five fish would be a chore, and it was difficult to scale the fish with a knife. The last item on the list was the bamboo poles. The tip of the pole had to be just right; it was the key to catching fish. Bamboo poles were seven to eight feet long, and cost $1.25. The flexible tip was thirty inches, and if the tip got broken, the fisherman had to replace the pole.

As they turned to leave the garage Jimmy's eye caught a glimpse of his brother's casting rod and reel. The rod brought back a bad memory from last year. Mr. Robinson and Jimmy's brother fished with a casting rod and reel. They used artificial lures (plugs that wiggled in the water with two sets of hooks). His brother Hugh got a new casting rod and reel in November for his thirteenth birthday. The following April he was practicing on the front lawn, casting a plug at a round circle on the ground. Before his brother went in the house he warned Jimmy not to touch the rod that he left standing against the tree. Jimmy watched his brother disappear into the house and he was anxious to try the new rod. He had to be quick; his brother would smack him if he caught him with the new rod. Jimmy picked up the rod, thinking casting couldn't be that hard. He reared back and gave a mighty cast, but nothing happened; the line didn't go out. He remembered his brother doing something with a button on the side of the reel before he cast. He found the button on the side of the reel and released it. The line was free to move and he reared back with arms extended and cast the plug high in the air. Unfortunately his direction was off and the plug landed on the roof of the house. He gave the line a tug, but the hooks were firmly embedded in the shingle. He started to panic, remembering that his brother told him not to touch the rod. A quick jerk of the rod didn't help. He reeled some of the line in and jerked with all his strength. Without warning, the plug released from the shingle and flew back over his head. His heart was racing and he experienced a sense of relief. The happiness was short-lived when the plug flew back to the rod and hooked him in the back of the head. "Ouch!" That hurt. Jimmy could feel the plug with his hand, but the hooks were buried in the nape of his neck. After several efforts to remove the plug he started to cry. His neck hurt, and he didn't know what to do. "I'm in big trouble," he thought, and he screamed for help.

His mother and brother came running out of the house. They looked at Jimmy and started to laugh. His mother tried to remove the hooks, but thought she might only further injure her son. His brother removed the plug from the line. "I told you not to touch the rod!"

Union Lake didn't have a doctor, but the Tuberculosis Sanitarium was nearby, and had a doctor. Jimmy's mother decided to take him there. A young doctor examined Jimmy while he told his story. "Next time you'll listen to your brother before you use his things, right? But I can remove the plug and you'll be fine." The doctor shaved the back of Jimmy's neck and removed the plug. It hurt, but Jimmy bit his lip and didn't cry. When he got home, Roger and his brother Ron were there to greet him. They laughed when they heard his story. "Pretty soon everybody will know, and they'll all be laughing at me," thought Jimmy.

As they walked around the house, Roger looke
roof and started to laugh. "Remember when you hool
head? That was really funny."

"At least I tried to cast. Someday I'll be a good caster; just you wait and see."

Roger said, "We still have enough time to go to Marohn's. Let's buy our gear, and if we have any money left over we can get a Mounds Bar."

They both liked coconut, but Jimmy preferred the Almond Joy. If they couldn't agree, they would settle the dispute by flipping a coin. Marohn's Grocery Store was a ten-minute walk away, but it would take at least twenty minutes. They walked on Union Lake road along the bay and stopped to skip stones on the water. Jimmy had the record, nine skips. The secret was finding a flat stone about two to three inches in diameter. The roadside gravel was too small and seldom offered the proper stone. Wherever the boys walked or played they were always looking for the perfect stone. They would usually have two or three stones in their pocket to skip on the way to the store. The willow tree with its large canopy sheltered the water from the wind and it was a good place to skip stones. The water was rough today and neither boy had a good stone. The fishing site was located between the store and the willow tree and the gravel parking lot offered a variety of stones. Roger said, "If I can get the right stone and a perfect throw I'll beat your record. If you catch the top of the wave just right, the stone will skip forever."

Jimmy took a closer look at the water in the bay and he saw the heads of several Leatherback Turtles bobbing in the waves. "The water is too rough; you're wasting your time."

They entered the store and headed to the rear where the fishing gear was displayed. The supply was limited, but all they needed were the basics. The bamboo poles were outside in a rack, and they could pick their own. Jimmy was eyeing the casting rods. "When I'm thirteen I'll have one," he thought.

Mr. Marohn was behind the counter. Jimmy read from their list. "We need a package of mixed hooks and a package of sinkers. Two round bobbers, two cone-shaped bobbers, a fish stringer and two bamboo poles. We only have six dollars, how much have we spent?"

Mr. Marohn added up the items on the cash register. "You've spent $4.90; you still have $1.10 left."

Roger said, "Jimmy forgot the line and the fish scaler. Can we get those too?"

"The line costs $.75 and the scaler is $.50; you can have both of them and pay me tomorrow. I'll pay you a dollar if you'll come tomorrow and clean up behind the store. It shouldn't take more than two hours. That's pretty good pay for boys your age. Since Bud joined the Army, I never have enough time."

It sounded good to Jimmy and Roger was nodding his head. "We'll come back tomorrow. Can we get a large Mounds Bar today?"

Mr. Marohn laughed, saying, "If I'm going to trust you for fifteen cents, I can handle another dime."

Jimmy inquired, "Have you heard from Bud? Is he all right?"

"He's all right. Bud's training in England. The allied forces are getting ready to invade France. I don't think that will happen until next year."

"How many times have you seen the big turtle?" Jimmy was curious.

"When I was a boy I might have seen a big turtle two or three times. You can't be sure it's the same turtle; there's probably more than one. This was farmland when I was growing up, and few people used the lake. The Leatherback Turtles would be on logs and on the banks sunning themselves. There were a lot of big turtles, and some were bigger than others. Most of the cottages were built after the first war in the 1920's, before you boys were born. I haven't seen a big turtle in years. Bud said he saw one on the corner of the fishing site near the willow tree. He probably comes in the early morning to sun his back. I mentioned the turtle to Mr. Robinson, and he said he's never seen him. It's a big lake and you may never see that turtle again. I'll see you boys tomorrow after lunch."

"We'll be here," replied Roger.

On the way home they stopped at the fishing site. It was really a public boat launch that anybody could use. It had a sloped gravel ramp to launch boats and adequate parking space for fifteen or twenty cars with trailers. Since the war, few fishermen had the time or the gas to use the fishing site. On the corner there was a half-dead willow tree that jutted out into shallow water. The tree was partially uprooted, and for ten feet it was almost parallel to the ground and water. Boaters would use the tree to tie up their boat. The beach surrounding the tree was gently sloped and the water was shallow. A turtle could easily make its way onto land at that spot.

CHAPTER FOUR

The Day Before

There was much to do before the opening day of fishing season. They would need to dig at least thirty worms and catch some minnows. Jimmy and Roger lived in the three-block area between Union Lake and Long Lake, referred to as the double privilege neighborhood. Residents had access to both lakes through four community lots, or privilege lots. There were two lots on each lake, and Jimmy's boat was docked at privilege lot one on Union Lake. Lot one was swampy with rich black dirt, an ideal place to dig for worms. They were disappointed when they arrived at the lot; someone had been digging the day before. There were worms to be had, but they needed to dig between tree roots and in the heavy grass. After digging for two hours, they had twenty-nine worms, and the worms

23

weren't very big. Roger dropped the shovel and rubbed his sore hands. "The people who dug worms yesterday got all the big ones. We'll never get enough worms, and my hands hurt. Do you want to try to catch minnows?"

"Did you bring the bread?"

"My mother gave me some stale bread to make breadcrumbs."

Catching minnows was a new experience. They walked out on the dock and Jimmy put the net in shallow water. Roger crushed the bread in his hands and floated the breadcrumbs on the surface to attract the minnows.

A few small minnows started to nibble the bread and strayed over the net. Jimmy tugged hard, but the minnows swam away before the net surfaced.

"You pulled the net too soon. We need to have more minnows over the net to catch them."

"Let's try over here. The water isn't as deep and you can tell me when to pull up." Jimmy lowered the net into the water and Roger scattered the breadcrumbs. Six or seven minnows nibbled at the bread. Jimmy wanted to pull the net, but he wasn't sure. Two minnows swam away.

Roger tugged on Jimmy's arm, "Pull the net up."

Jimmy pulled and there were two minnows. They caught eight more minnows before they ran out of bread. Minnows needed fresh water to stay alive. Yesterday Roger punched holes in a large coffee can to circulate the water. Jimmy put a rock in the can and placed it in shallow water under the dock for the next morning.

Jimmy was laughing, and said, "I think you're going to owe Ron a quarter. We're not going to have enough bait to catch twenty-five fish. Those little bluegills steal our worms and we've never fished with minnows."

"Don't be so sure. Maybe I can catch some night crawlers tonight. If I'm lucky, I might get five. They're big, and we can break them in pieces. Five night crawlers are the same as twenty worms."

Night crawlers were large worms that came out after dark to cool their body on the damp lawn. You needed a flashlight to spot them and quick hands to catch them, but they were worth the effort. Jimmy wasn't quick enough to grab the first night crawler before it retreated back into the ground. Roger's small stature and quick hands made him an even match for the night crawler and he caught more than he missed. The night crawler was too big for the small pan fish Jimmy and Roger caught, and so they would break the worms into smaller pieces to bait their hooks. The boys parted at Roger's home. Jimmy said, "I'll be here at five-thirty. We need to have our lines in the water when the sun comes up."

"That's really early, but I'll be ready. I want to win my bet with Ron."

Jimmy was quiet during dinner, as he could only think of catching fish. After dinner he checked his pole; everything was in order. His father got up at six, but Jimmy wanted to be up by five. The house was small and he was sure to wake the others. No one in the family wanted to get up at five. His father finally agreed to rise at five-thirty. Jimmy called Roger; he would be there at six. His brother was fishing for bass with a friend on Cooley Lake and they were starting at seven. Jimmy tossed and turned, and finally went to sleep at ten.

CHAPTER FIVE

Opening Day

Jimmy didn't need an alarm clock or his father's help; he was up before five-thirty. He ate a bowl of corn flakes and strawberries, and made a peanut butter and jelly sandwich for lunch. As he was leaving his brother and father were sitting down for breakfast. His father liked fresh fish and he wished Jimmy and his brother good luck. At Roger's house, the kitchen light was on. Roger greeted him with a smile, he was anxious to win his bet. They loaded their gear in Roger's red wagon and headed for the privilege lot. As they approached the boat dock, they could see car lights across the bay at the fishing site. The fishermen were busy launching their boats. The sun was rising over the horizon and there was little cloud cover. The coffee can with the holes did the trick, and their minnows were alive.

Roger put the can in a pail of fresh water and placed the pail under the seat to keep the minnows from the morning sun. King jumped in the boat and Roger pushed off from the dock. Jimmy rowed to their favorite spot near the willow tree, Roger dropped the anchor on the edge of the drop-off, and they were ready.

Roger reached for the minnows. "I got four night-crawlers last night. My father said to have a worm on one pole and a minnow on the other pole."

"I don't think that will work, since we don't have enough minnows. If you're going to win your bet with Ron we should both fish with the worms and night crawlers. If you waste time with the minnows you'll miss the early catch. If we're going to get twenty-five fish, we'll have to catch most of them by ten o'clock."

"I want to win that quarter; I'll fish with the worms and night crawlers."

"We can use the minnows when we run out of worms. You fish on the deep side and I'll fish off the back of the boat." Jimmy adjusted his bobber, and threw the line in the water. It didn't take long; the bobber disappeared under the water. Jimmy caught the first fish, an eight-inch rock bass.

"Wow, that's a big rock bass." Roger watched his bobber go down, and he hooked a perch before Jimmy had his fish on the stringer. With two stringers, they could determine who caught the most fish. It was important for bragging rights, as last year they weren't sure. They fished at a steady pace for the next three hours. Jimmy baited his hook with a piece of a night crawler. He threw the line in the water and braced his pole under the seat. "I wonder how many fish we've caught; these little bluegills are stealing our worms."

Roger nodded his head. "I've caught more little fish than keepers. Let's count them, I think I'm ahead."

They pulled their stringers and counted the fish. Roger had seven and Jimmy had six. Neither had a watch, but a boat was passing nearby. Jimmy asked the time. It was almost nine. He looked at the sun; nine was about right, he figured.

"Let's move toward the dock and get away from these bluegills. Leave your line in the water and pull up the anchor."

Roger nodded his approval as Jimmy's bobber disappeared under the water. Jimmy reached for his pole; he could tell by the feel that it wasn't a small fish. There was twenty feet of line on the pole, and the fish was at the end of the line. He pulled the pole up, and the bent tip formed a semi-circle; it looked like the tip would break. Jimmy struggled to bring the fish to the boat, but the line was too long, the fish was too heavy, and the pole was too short. The fish was still hooked and it jumped twenty feet from the boat. Roger stood up waving his arms and shouting advice; he almost fell out of the boat. "Put your pole down and bring the line in with your hands." The excitement startled King and he put his front feet on the side of the boat and started to bark.

"Sit down, you're gonna fall out of the boat."

Roger took King by the collar and sat down.

Jimmy went hand over hand toward the end of the pole. When he reached the tip he grabbed the line and dropped the pole in the water. Free of the pole, he pulled on the line with both hands. Without the flex of the pole it was hard to keep tension on the line. The fish fought gamely and the line cut into the boy's hands. Roger offered to help, but Jimmy wanted to catch the fish on his own. He pulled harder on the line and wrapped it around his left hand. The fish jumped a second time; it had to be two feet long.

Jimmy stood up in the boat and braced his legs, certain this fish wasn't going to get away. With a determined look in his eye, he renewed his struggle with the big fish. Several minutes passed and the fish jumped a third time. Jimmy sensed that the fish was tiring and he slowly advanced the line toward the boat. First came the bobber; then he could see the fish in the water. It was important that the fish not bang the side of the boat and loosen the hook. The fish had stopped fighting as it neared the boat, and Jimmy reached in the water and grabbed the line near the mouth of the fish. He got a firm hold on the line and lifted the big bass into the boat. It was by far the biggest fish he had ever caught. King barked as the bass thrashed about the bottom of the boat. Roger and Jimmy measured their fish with a stick marked at six inches for the small fish and ten inches for the bass they hoped to catch. Roger tried to measure the fish as it thrashed about. He was in awe. "That's a monster bass, and I think it's fifteen inches long. It looked just like the magazine picture when it jumped out of the water." He used both hands to pick the fish up, "I'll bet it weighs three pounds."

Lucky for Jimmy, the big bass had swallowed the hook. Had the fish been hooked in the mouth, it might have gotten away when it jumped. Jimmy cut the line and put the fish on his stringer. His heart was pounding, and his hands were shaking as he tied a new hook on his line. Everyone knew that the biggest bass ever caught in Union Lake was eighteen inches. Two summers ago Bud caught a sixteen-inch bass, and it was the biggest bass he had ever caught. Jimmy experienced a new sense of pride.

Roger shouted, "I got one," it was another perch. "Let's move closer to the dock."

The fish had stopped biting and the new spot had more little bluegills. Jimmy could tell by the sun that it was approaching noon, and it was time to count their catch. They lifted the stringers, Roger had ten fish and Jimmy had nine. It was a good catch, and more fish than they had caught last year, but Roger would lose the bet to his brother Ron. They were out of worms and they seldom caught fish in the afternoon. Roger shook his head, "We don't have enough minnows to catch six more fish. These little bluegills got most of our worms. I must have caught ten that I threw back."

"Me too. We caught more little fish than we did keepers. It's time for lunch, let's go to the fishing site and see how the other boats did."

They put their fish in a pail of fresh water, and Jimmy rowed to the fishing site. Several boats were tied to the old willow tree and two more were on the beach. Fishermen like to talk, particularly about the number of fish caught and the size of the fish. One man was showing a fourteen-inch small mouth bass and a woman had a fifteen-inch large-mouth bass. They were taking pictures when one of the men asked Jimmy how he had done.

Jimmy fetched his stringer from the boat and with both arms he raised his catch. The man was surprised, saying, "How did you land that big bass with a bamboo pole? Do you boys have a net?"

"The fish swallowed the hook. I put my pole in the water and pulled the line in with my hands, and no, we don't have a net."

The woman smiled at Jimmy. "That was quite a feat. Is that your first big bass?"

"Yes, ma'am."

"This is a special day for you. Let me take your picture, and I'll mail it to you."

Jimmy and Roger held their stringers up, with Jimmy's bass properly displayed.

The woman wrote down Jimmy's address and said, "It takes a week to process the film, so you'll have the pictures in two weeks."

Jimmy replied, "Thank you, ma'am, that would mean a lot to me. Our camera is broken and my mom can't find a new one she likes."

"Someday the war will be over and life will be like it used to be. Don't worry, I'll send your pictures."

Jimmy said to Roger, "We have to go home and clean the fish. They'll die and start to smell if we're not quick about it."

Jimmy put the minnows under the dock and they placed the fish in two pails of fresh water. The gear and the fish went in Roger's red wagon and they headed to Jimmy's house to clean their fish. The best place to clean fish was in the shade of the large maple tree in the backyard. Jimmy got two pans and a cake of ice from his mother while Roger pulled the hose under the tree. Jimmy's mother had ordered an extra block of ice in anticipation of a large catch. Pan fish spoiled quickly if they weren't properly iced. They cleaned the big bass first. The stomach had a partially digested minnow and Jimmy retrieved the hook. They worked as a team, one scaling and the other gutting the fish. They cleaned Jimmy's fish first and then traded places. It took over an hour, but the fish scaler helped. Jimmy's mother came out the back door with two glasses of lemonade. She was impressed with the catch. Jimmy's brother had caught two small bass and the family would be eating fish for several days. Roger thanked her for the lemonade.

Jimmy asked his mother, "Can we go fishing this afternoon? We want to try our minnows."

"How about you go right now; I want you home for a fish dinner at six. Then it's off to bed; you boys were up early this morning."

It was after two o'clock, and they could fish for a couple more hours. The boys could tell the time by the sun, and were seldom off by more than thirty minutes. They stopped at Roger's house to deliver his fish, and Roger grabbed a shovel, as they needed more worms. Jimmy dug feverishly, but his effort produced only four worms and they were running out of time.

Roger shook his head, saying, "We'd better get fishing, since there aren't any worms here."

Roger wanted to fish in deeper water. They selected a spot near the dock and anchored the boat past the weeds on the edge of the drop-off. The deeper water required more line and they needed to adjust their bobbers. Jimmy was measuring the line with his arm; it appeared to be fifteen feet deep, about eight feet deeper than this morning. At long last, it was time to try their minnows. It was important to hook the minnow just right. Properly hooked, the minnow would continue to move and attract the fish. Roger had small hands and he carefully baited both hooks. With their lines in the water they waited patiently for the bobbers to move, but nothing happened. After twenty minutes they pulled their lines, the minnows were dead. Roger carefully baited the hooks and they placed the lines in the water. Minutes later Roger had a strike; his bobber went straight down. The tip of the bamboo pole was bent and the line was going back and forth in the water, but Roger couldn't move the fish. Unlike Jimmy's big fish, the line was straight down, and the fish didn't surface to jump.

Jimmy was quick to encourage his friend. "Hang on; it looks like a big one."

"Really big; I'm not strong enough to get it in the boat."

"My brother said that pike don't jump like bass. Remember that turtle I caught, it didn't feel like a fish. Give me the pole and bring the line in with your hands."

Roger handed Jimmy the pole; whatever was on the line was heavy. He swung the pole over the rear of the boat and adjusted the length so Roger could reach the line. Several minutes passed and Roger wasn't making any progress. He looked at Jimmy to say, "The line is slippery and I can't pull it up. Give me the pole and you pull the line."

"If I help you, it's not the same. Wrap the line around your hand and pull with both hands. If the fish swallowed the hook; you're not going to lose it. If you keep at it you'll tire him out."

Roger followed Jimmy's advice and slowly he raised the fish. "I can see the bobber." Then he shouted, "You should see the size of this fish, I think it's a Northern Pike."

Jimmy put the pole down and moved to Roger's side, watching the fish thrashing about in the water; it wasn't going to get away. Northern Pike had a long snout with two rows of sharp teeth. You could hurt your hand if it got caught in the fish's mouth.

Jimmy was trying to think of a way to get the fish into the boat. The boat was close to the shore and he remembered a story where a man landed a shark by moving his boat into shallow water and beaching the fish. "Give the fish more line and I'll row toward the shore. You can go into the shallow water and get him."

"Can you believe it? I've caught a three-foot fish! Wait till Ron sees this one."

Jimmy pulled up the anchor and headed toward the shore. He beached the boat and Roger triumphantly lifted the fish out of the water. He was careful to avoid the Northern Pike's sharp teeth when he put the fish on his stringer. The fish was almost as tall as he was. "I did it, Jimmy, I caught the fish by myself."

They put their gear and the pike in Roger's wagon and headed for home. His brother Ron smiled at Roger with pride as he measured the fish; it was thirty-three inches long. "It's a big fish, but you still owe me a quarter. I'm not letting you cut it into six pieces."

They all laughed and Roger slugged Jimmy on the shoulder. "We did it, Jimmy, we did it. I knew we could catch bigger fish if we had a boat and some minnows. This is the best day of my life; I caught the most fish and the biggest fish."

"You sure did, I never thought you'd catch a bigger fish than mine. We better clean it right now and pack it in ice. Hugh says that pike get fishy real quick when they're out of the water. The sooner you eat them the better they taste."

CHAPTER SIX

The Next Week

Jerry's mother called to say the family wouldn't open the cottage until the Fourth of July weekend. They didn't have enough gas coupons to make the trip in June. Jimmy was disappointed, he wanted to explore the big bay the other side of the point, and he wanted Jerry to go with him. Roger had little interest in the rest of the lake; he was content to stay in the bay. Jimmy's birthday was on Wednesday, and nothing special was planned. His mother promised to make meatloaf with mashed potatoes and a chocolate cake, Jimmy's favorite meal.

After the opening day of fishing season, there was little activity on the lake until the Fourth of July weekend. It was nice to be the only boat on the lake and Jimmy wanted to go fishing on Monday. Roger said no, he wanted to sleep in.

On Sunday afternoon Jimmy dug through the mulch pile looking for worms. He was anxious to be on his own and the only boat on the lake. His father promised to wake him and he had King to keep him company.

The air was warming in the bright sunshine and the water was calm when he pushed off from the dock. As he turned the boat he saw something move on the fishing site next to the willow tree. What did Mr. Marohn say? "Bud saw a big turtle on the fishing site near the willow tree." Jimmy turned in his seat and faced the front of the boat to watch the area. He slowly advanced the boat without disturbing the morning calm. Halfway there, he could see the big turtle basking in the morning sun with head and feet tucked securely in its shell. He pushed gently on the oars and let the boat drift as it neared the fishing site. He compared the turtle to a big rock ten feet away. The rock looked to be two feet wide, and the turtle was the same size. The turtle fascinated him, and he sat motionless for twenty minutes. Suddenly a car pulled in on the loose gravel and frightened the turtle. The head emerged and the flipper-like legs and claws scattered the gravel and sand as the turtle headed toward the water. The rear legs were powerful, but it was obvious that the turtle moved slowly on land. Once in the water, the turtle quickly disappeared. Minutes later Jimmy's heart was still pounding. He took a deep breath, the turtle was gone and it was time to fish. Jimmy had caught four fish, but he couldn't stop thinking about the turtle.

After lunch Jimmy and the Clark boys went swimming in Long Lake. Most of the neighborhood kids went swimming every day, and the group ranged in age from seven to thirteen. They had a large community raft, and their favorite pastime was pushing each other off the raft. The bigger kids had an advantage; it took two smaller kids to push them off. The girls enjoyed pushing the boys off. Occasionally someone got hurt and went home crying.

Jimmy couldn't wait to tell about the turtle. His friends listened to every word. Jimmy concluded his story by saying, "I want to catch the turtle." The others laughed. If the turtle was as big as Jimmy said it was, there was no way to catch it. They didn't have a rifle to shoot the turtle; they only had Ron's BB gun. Ron advised him, "Forget the turtle, Jimmy, it's baseball season and we need to practice if we're going to play the kids from Westacres. They're better than us because they have more kids and a better field to practice on. We need to fill in the holes and cut the grass on our field before we can practice. If we're going to beat them we need to get started today; our first practice is next week."

Union Lake didn't have enough boys aged ten to twelve to field a baseball team. Other boys from the surrounding communities and the boys from Detroit joined the team and this year they would have twelve players. The baseball field was a vacant lot across from the bus stop, and it took two days to mow the field with push mowers. Ron had some of the other boys on the team coming tomorrow to help fill the holes and cut the grass. Regardless of their effort, ground balls would take strange hops in the infield and occasionally balls hit to the outfield would get lost in the long grass.

That night Jimmy lay awake in his bed. He was trying to figure out a plan to catch the big turtle. If he could only hide from the turtle; but there was no place to hide on the fishing site, and running on the gravel would scare the turtle.

The next morning he was up early, and his mother sent him to the store to buy bread. King would bark at the turtle so he left him in the garage. As he neared the fishing site he spotted the big turtle next to the willow tree. The turtle was basking in the sun close to the water's edge. There was a clump of bushes in the corner by the road. Jimmy slowly made his way along the road and hid behind the bushes. He was quiet and observed the turtle. The head and feet were tucked securely in the shell and the turtle appeared to be sleeping. Jimmy analyzed the terrain. "If I move quietly along the edge of the water, I could sneak up on the turtle." As Jimmy was planning his attack, the turtle came out of its shell and slowly made its way to the water. The head and flipper front feet were huge and the claws on the rear legs looked threatening. "If I jump on the turtle's back and stay away from its back feet and head, the turtle can't hurt me."

The turtle was big, but he was bigger. If Roger helped, the two of them could put the turtle in a wash tub.

Jimmy headed to the store, and Mr. Marohn was at the counter. "I just saw the big turtle. He was next to the old willow tree. He's got this huge neck and head and lies there in the sun every day."

"Slow down, Jimmy, I can't understand you."

Jimmy took a deep breath. "I hid in the bushes and watched the big turtle. He just lies there, I think he's sleeping. When he started to go in the water, he stuck his head out. His head and neck are huge."

"You probably saw something that few people have seen up close. I looked up soft shell turtles in the Encyclopedia. It's probably a female turtle; they're larger than the male. The female turtle has to be large, because her eggs are large, and she will lay as many as thirty-five eggs. Fresh water Leatherback Turtles live to be fifty years old. Now tell me the truth; how big is she?"

"She's as big as that rock on the bank." Jimmy spread his arms wide. "About this big."

"Bud said the turtle he saw was two feet wide. She's an exception; few Leatherbacks reach that size. They make good soup and that one could weigh forty pounds, and that's a lot of turtle soup. How close did you get?"

"I was in the bushes next to the road. It's about the same distance as running to first base. Yesterday a car pulled into the parking area and spooked the turtle. It was throwing gravel with its flippers, but the turtle isn't very fast on land."

"With everyone working in the defense plants, there's little activity at the fishing site. The turtle must feel safe or it wouldn't be on land. I think the Leatherbacks spend most of their time in the bay. The bluff east of the fishing site has soft sand and they like to lie in the sun and bury themselves in the soft sand. The female digs a hole in the sand and lays her eggs at night. Their front legs are large flippers with claws; they're good for swimming and digging. The rear legs are smaller and stronger and they have sharp claws. The turtle pushes with the rear legs to walk on land and uses a swimming motion with the front legs. Their front legs can't support them and they drag their shell on the ground. If someone says you're moving at a 'turtle's pace' it means you're slow."

"That's how she was walking. Last year I dove off the boat to catch a Leatherback. They can really swim fast."

"Much faster than you can, that's why those front flippers are so big. That bluff might be the place where they lay their eggs, but don't go there and disturb the ground. That's ten cents, Jimmy."

"I wondered where all those turtles came from; some days there must be twenty turtles in the bay."

Jimmy stopped at the fishing site on the way home. He walked from the bushes to where the turtle was; it was closer to eighty feet. If he ran fast, he could jump on the turtle's back. With Rogers's help his plan would work. Maybe they could sell the turtle? Mr. Marohn said they made turtle soup from Leatherback Turtles. Jimmy was concentrating so hard he didn't see his brother approaching on his bike. His brother was mad. "Why are you fooling around? Mother needs the bread to make our lunches."

Jimmy handed his brother the bread, saying, "I'm sorry, I didn't mean to hold you up."

After lunch, Jimmy and Roger went swimming in Long Lake. "I got up early today and saw the big turtle. I snuck up and hid in those bushes along the road. The turtle likes to lie in the sun next to the willow tree. Mr. Marohn said it's a female and they're bigger than the male turtle. Baby turtles are like baby chicks; they come from eggs. She's not very fast on land. Her legs are like flippers with claws, the turtle kind of swims instead of walking."

"The turtle just lies there? Did it see you?"

"No, I never moved and her head is inside the shell. I measured the distance from the bushes to where the turtle was; it's about eighty feet. I think we can catch the turtle. Mr. Marohn says the turtle weighs forty pounds, and they use Leatherback Turtles for turtle soup. I figured it out. If we get five cents a pound, that's two dollars."

"We can't catch a turtle that big. Don't you remember what happened last summer when that little Leatherback bit you? A turtle that big could bite your finger off. I'd rather go fishing and try to catch another pike. Let's catch some minnows and fish in that same spot tomorrow morning."

"Tomorrow's my birthday and I need your help to catch the turtle. Remember the big snow? I helped you shovel the driveway on your birthday. We'll need your mother's wash tub and some gloves so the turtle can't scratch us. We'll hide in the bushes and, when the turtle falls asleep,

I'll run and jump on her back. You can bring the tub, and if we pick the turtle up between her feet, she can't scratch or bite us. I'm bigger than the turtle; she can't drag me in the water."

"I'll get a spanking if my mother needs the tub. Why don't we use your mother's tub? Your father doesn't spank as hard as my father does."

Jimmy was using the tub as a bargaining chip. Now Roger would have to help him if they used his mother's tub. "We can use our tub, but you have to help me. It's my birthday, Roger, and I want to do something special. Don't be a chicken and let me down."

"I'll help, but we have to use your tub. I'll be ready, but if I get scratched or that turtle bites me it's your fault. We should leave that turtle alone."

CHAPTER SEVEN

The Catch

Jimmy had large hands and an old pair of his brother's work gloves proved to be a good fit. He put the gloves in the wash tub. They needed to run fast and Roger suggested they wear their bathing suits. After dinner he asked his father to wake him early and his dad shook his head. "We don't need any more fish, Jimmy; I'm tired of eating fish."

"I'm not going fishing for the small fish; I'm going to try to catch another bass. I'll give the fish to the people next door if we can't eat it.

"I'm sure they'll appreciate it. Your mother wants some froglegs for Saturday's dinner; we'll go frogging Friday night.

Jimmy nodded his head; he could barely contain himself.

He woke up with his father and had a bowl of cereal for breakfast. King looked at Jimmy with sorrowful eyes; he didn't like being left in the garage. Jimmy breathed a sigh of relief; the light was on at Roger's house. The sun was up as they pushed off from the dock. There weren't any cars at the fishing site; it was calm and peaceful.

The turtle wasn't there when they beached the boat. Jimmy knelt on the lakeside of the bushes, and Roger was on the beach side. The ground was sloping toward the water and Jimmy tried to get comfortable. It seemed like an eternity but it was probably closer to thirty minutes and the turtle hadn't appeared. Roger was fidgety, and said, "The turtle isn't coming, let's get some minnows and go fishing for pike."

"It's my birthday and you promised to help me catch the turtle, so we can wait a while longer."

"I'll wait fifteen more minutes, then I'm going."

Jimmy's leg had fallen asleep in the cramped position and he stood up to get the blood flowing. Just as he was hunkering down again, the turtle emerged from the water and started up the bank. She turned slowly back toward the water and settled at the water's edge with her feet and head tucked securely in her shell. Jimmy's heart started to beat faster and Roger tugged at his arm and whispered, "She sure is big, I don't think the tub is big enough."

"Hush up, you'll scare her."

They waited patiently for the turtle to fall asleep before launching their charge. Jimmy's mouth felt dry as he realized that the time had come to execute his perfect plan. Roger elbowed him in the ribs, it was time to go. Jimmy tugged at his gloves and looked at Roger for approval when both were startled by a loud bang from a backfiring car. The noise spooked the turtle and she moved toward the water. Jimmy scrambled to his feet and headed for the turtle, but it was too late. All he saw was her powerful flippers propelling rocks and sand as she headed for the water. As he approached the turtle was swimming to the safety of the drop-off. Roger was close behind with the wash tub.

Jimmy looked at Roger, "What was that noise; it scared the snot out of me."

"It was a car backfiring, probably the Reynolds kid in his Ford. We missed our chance, she'll never come here again, there's too much going on."

That night at dinner, Jimmy's mother made a chocolate cake for his birthday. After they sang happy birthday and devoured the cake, Jimmy's brother and sister gave him a special gift. It was a large box, but it wasn't something large, it was a new baseball glove. Jimmy smiled his appreciation as he pounded the pocket to break the glove in. His parents gave him a new sweatshirt and his grandparents gifted him a new pair of pants. He was happy with his presents but he had an empty feeling. He would gladly forsake his gifts for one more opportunity to catch the big turtle. He knew his chances were slim, but he wasn't giving up. Bud had seen the big turtle at the fishing site and he had seen the turtle there two times. She liked the beach and the warm sun. If he got a second chance he would catch her.

CHAPTER EIGHT

Cutting Grass

Jimmy was up early Thursday morning; he had two lawns to cut. He was thankful that a family friend had accompanied him and showed him how to adjust the blades on the push mowers so they made a clean cut. It was difficult to mow a lawn without hitting a rock or a stick and knocking the mower out of adjustment. Jimmy was pushing the mower up a hill when he hit a small rock that stopped the mower. He removed the rock and checked the cut; the mower wasn't cutting on the right side. He took his screwdriver and turned the adjustment screw. If the mower cut paper, it would cut the grass. He checked the cut with a strip of newspaper; the mower was tearing at the paper. He adjusted the right screw down one turn and moved the left screw up a half turn. He checked again, the mower was now cutting the paper and the reel was moving freely.

Jimmy was happy cutting grass, and he enjoyed being outside and earning his own money. Next spring he would purchase a new Schwinn bike and try to get a paper route. You were supposed to be twelve to get a paper route, but he was big for his age. This weekend he was going to caddie at the golf course. The caddy master said he was too young, but he was unable to get the older boys to do it. Jimmy wasn't big enough to carry double (two bags), but he had no problem with a single bag. Roger wasn't five feet tall and weighed less than one hundred pounds; he was too small to caddie. His friend Jerry from Detroit didn't need to caddy; he got a dollar a week allowance. Jimmy loved to play golf, and caddies got to play free on Mondays. He had an old set of rusted ladies clubs, and he needed a better set of clubs if he was going to improve his game.

He was thinking ahead, and there were several expensive items on his wish list. The bike cost $25.00 and a set of used golf clubs could cost as much as $30.00, he estimated. He had outgrown his school jacket, and a new jacket cost $7.00 or so. Sneakers cost $3.00, and his were tight and wearing out. He was growing so fast that his clothes only lasted one season before they had to be replaced. His brother's old clothes were too big and he needed to earn enough money to buy new clothes for school. The thought of all that money made him more determined, and he pushed harder on the mower. "I forgot the hockey skates. Maybe I'll get the hockey skates for Christmas."

CHAPTER NINE

Frogging

Jimmy's family liked froglegs. They were better than chicken and plentiful during the summer months. The big dark green bullfrogs had the largest legs and there was an ample supply along the south shore of Long Lake bordering the golf course. Jimmy's dad had purchased an old wooden canoe last winter and spent the spring refurbishing it. The canoe was long and narrow and easy to tip; so they named it TIPPACANOE. It was painted canary yellow and accented with a bright red stripe along the top. The interior was a beautiful mahogany wood with several coats of marine varnish. Jimmy's father was a commercial artist, and he lettered TIPPACANOE on both sides. The family docked their boat on Union Lake and the canoe was docked on Long Lake. The old canoe was heavy, but it was the fastest canoe on the lake. Jimmy and his brother Hugh could paddle TIPPACANOE across Long Lake and back with little effort.

Jimmy had started to go frogging with his dad the summer of last year, but they needed to borrow a boat and only went two or three times. The south shore on Long Lake was shallow with cattails, reeds and lily pads that decorated the surface of the water. His father wore hip boots, not to keep his legs dry, but to protect his feet and legs from the sharp objects below and above the water line. When it was dark, they paddled to the East End of the reeds and worked west. The shoreline bordered the fourth hole and the sixteenth hole on the golf course. Golfers often hit their balls in the water and occasionally Jimmy's father would step on a golf ball or spot one in the water. Jimmy used the balls when he played golf on Monday.

His father used a flashlight and a three-prong spear. He would walk slowly, criss-crossing a path from the shore to the outer perimeter of the reeds using the light to spot the frogs. The male bullfrogs made a croaking sound that was helpful in locating them. The bright light hypnotized the frog, and Jimmy's father would then spear it. This year,

Jimmy followed in the canoe a few feet behind his father. He would remove the frog from the spear and put it in a burlap bag packed with ice. They started after dark and it took two hours to work the south shore. They were out an hour when Jimmy's father asked, "How many frogs do we have?"

"We've got eleven; I've been keeping count. We've got some big ones, but we need more."

His father remarked, "We're only half way through, the biggest frogs are ahead of us."

Jimmy's father bent over and headed toward shore. Whammo! He had another frog. Jimmy removed the frog and his father went back to work. Suddenly the flashlight went into the air and it seemed like his father was falling. There was a commotion and Jimmy felt something strike him on the shoulder. It spooked him, and he fell in the water, turning the canoe on its side. The water was shallow, and he quickly scrambled to his feet. His father retrieved his spear and headed for the canoe. Jimmy said, "Something hit me on the shoulder. It scared me and I fell out of the canoe."

"I stepped on a blue heron; they sleep standing up. It must have been a large one; it knocked me over when it took off. I'm still rattled; it scared the be-jebbers out of me."

Jimmy's father started to laugh. "I'm not sure who was scared more, me or the blue heron. Let's go to the shore so I can empty my boots and we can dump the water out of the canoe. Than its back to work, we need more frogs."

It was after eleven when they got home. Jimmy said goodnight and headed to bed. It took ten minutes to walk to the golf course, and he had to be there by eight. His mother would scold his father in the morning, admonishing him with, "Jimmy needs more sleep!"

Saturday night the family dined on French fried potatoes, coleslaw, and froglegs. Jimmy and his sister Iris spent Saturday afternoon picking wild strawberries. The desert was strawberry shortcake smothered in whipped cream. Wild strawberries were smaller and took longer to pick than the garden strawberries, but they were much sweeter, and that's why they took longer to pick. Jimmy would put one in the pot and two in his mouth. The family also had a good crop of strawberries they raised in their garden. The garden strawberries were larger and made excellent strawberry jam. One of the family's favorite deserts was strawberry-rhubarb pie.

On Monday Jimmy went to the grocery store for his mother. Mr. Marohn put the items in a bag as he addressed Jimmy. "Check with me next week, I'll need the back yard cleaned again. Have you caught any more bass or pike?"

"Not since opening day. My brother said it was beginners luck. Wednesday was my birthday and I wanted to do something special. Roger and I tried to catch the big turtle. I was going to jump on her back and hold her down till Roger got there with the wash tub. The turtle came while we were in the bushes, but a car backfired and scared her back into the water before we could grab her."

Mr. Marohn shook his head. "There's no law that says you can't catch a turtle, and there's no law that says a turtle can't bite your finger off or scratch your arms. If you jump on her, you'll be in one heck of a struggle; she'll be fighting for her life. The Leatherbacks like the bay because the food is plentiful and the drop-off is close to the shore. She might not return to the fishing site, since the eastern shore has a large sandy beach and there are no homes; it's a peaceful place for a turtle."

"Have you seen a big turtle there?"

"No. I'm like you, why go all over the lake when there's good fishing and a boat launch at this end of the lake. It's a big deep lake and there's probably more than one turtle of that size. They don't mingle together; you won't see two Leatherbacks sharing the same spot. You better stick to fishing; if you get your hands on of those big turtles your friends might be calling you three fingers." Mr. Marohn laughed and handed Jimmy the bag, "That's $1.05, please."

Jimmy was lost in thought on the way home. The east shore was two miles away; he had been there once in a speedboat. Without the benefit of a motor, he would have a difficult time exploring the east shore. Union Lake had two other bays on the west side of the lake, but neither had a good place for the turtle to bask in the morning sun. In late July, Jimmy's brother and Jerry's older brother accompanied them and they camped out on the east shore for two nights. The sandy beach was a perfect place to sun your back, but they didn't see any Leatherback Turtles. Jimmy's brother caught two bass on his casting rod. It was the first time they gone camping and Jimmy and Jerry enjoyed frying the fish over an open fire. Jerry burned his hand on the hot frying pan and his brother put some oil from the motor on the burn to ease the sting.

CHAPTER TEN

Hunting for Golf Balls

It was early August and Jimmy and Roger were walking home from the store. As was their practice, they stopped at the fishing site to collect stones to skip on the water. Jimmy looked at the spot next to the old willow tree where he had spotted the turtle. Since that fateful day he got up early once a week and hid in the bushes, but the turtle hadn't reappeared. Mr. Marohn was probably right, the turtle wouldn't return to the fishing site. Roger saw Jimmy staring at the willow tree. He had something else in mind and he wasn't sure if he could count on his friend. "I know how to make some money and have fun doing it."

"It can't be at Union Lake, I have to work hard to earn my money. It would be nice to have an allowance like Jerry gets, but our families haven't got the extra money."

"Everything costs so much because of the war, we'll never get an allowance. I'm not talking about cutting lawns and raking leaves, I'm talking about taking a chance like you did when you tried to catch the turtle. We get a few golf balls out of the lake, but everyone looks for balls along the shore."

"That's the only place you can look for balls without going on the golf course. They'll chase us off the course if we're caught looking for balls. John took the balls away from the kids he caught last week, and he called their parents to complain."

"We don't have to go all over the golf course to find balls. The pond on the third hole has hundreds of balls. Ron said the man who gets the balls from the pond is sick and he hasn't been here in two weeks. Ron said he gets over one hundred balls and they pay him ten dollars. We can get up early and sneak into the pond from Long Lake. If we get one hundred balls and sell them for ten cents each, that's ten dollars. We can set up a table next to the third tee on the other side of the fence and the golfers can look at the balls. We won't be on the golf course when we sell the balls."

Jimmy liked that part of Roger's plan. A friend from Cedar Island Lake sold golf balls on the third hole. He got twenty cents for the good balls, but he never had more than five balls. Because the third hole was over water, the golfers would buy older balls for a nickel or a dime so they wouldn't risk losing their good balls. He didn't feel right about going on the golf course without permission. "I earn fifty cents a week caddying. If I get caught in the pond John will be mad at me and he won't let me caddy. John cuts the greens early in the morning and he might see us."

"Ron said that John mows the greens on Tuesday and Thursday during the week, but tomorrow is Wednesday."

"No one goes in that pond, Roger, there's a bright red sign in the pond that says, 'DANGEROUS WATER.' There must be a good reason for the sign."

"You owe me Jimmy; I got up early to help you catch the turtle. I'm not big enough to caddy and I need money for a new jacket. Ron says the sign is there to keep the golfers from going into the water after their balls and slowing down play. Ron should know; he's the bus boy for the restaurant."

Jimmy caddied on Saturdays and Sundays, and he had no idea what went on during the week. Reluctantly he answered, "I'll go, but I don't feel good about it."

Roger clapped his hands with joy. "I'll pick you up before seven; we can walk there in ten minutes. Tell your parents we're going fishing, and wear your swim trunks under your clothes. Ron gave me two onion sacks to put the balls in. You won't chicken out?"

Jimmy shook his head, saying, "I won't chicken out."

Jimmy was putting King in the garage when Roger arrived. The golf course was a four-block walk, and they half-walked and half-ran along the shoreline of Long Lake to their destination. A ten-foot area covered with bushes and a willow tree separated the pond from Long Lake. They hung their clothes on a tree limb and waded into the water. They sank in the mucky bottom and decided to walk along the bank to the other side where most of the balls entered the water.

"Ron says the diver goes under the water and feels along the bottom. Let's separate, I'll start on the right side." Roger disappeared under the water.

Jimmy started to walk to his left and felt a ball with his foot. He picked up the ball. He took another step and there was another ball. Roger came up for air and he ordered Jimmy, "You'd better get started, we haven't got all day."

"There are balls along the shore and I can feel them with my feet. You look in the middle and I'll look here."

Roger nodded his head and again went underwater. Jimmy walked back and forth in the gooey muck along the bank, going into deeper water with each pass. They worked about an hour and Jimmy had filled half of his bag with golf balls. The water was up to his chest and his legs felt funny.

Roger came up for air. "I must have thirty balls. We should have close to a hundred if we work another hour."

"My legs feel funny; I'm going to the bank for a couple of minutes."

When Jimmy turned toward the bank, he spotted John coming down the hill. "You boys are trespassing; you're not supposed to be in the pond. That sign was put there for your protection. The man that fetches the balls wears a special suit to protect him from the leeches. Take a look at your legs; they're probably covered with leeches!"

Jimmy stepped out of the water. No wonder his legs felt funny; they were covered with bloodsuckers. Roger was close behind him and his body was covered with bloodsuckers. He was thrashing about in the water trying to shake them off.

"I'm not going to report you, but I have to take the balls. Don't try to pick those leeches off; there're too many, and the wounds could get infected from that dirty water. Go home and put salt on them and they'll fall off. When the leeches are gone, have your mother put iodine on the wounds. I suggest you take it easy the rest of the day." John turned to Jimmy. "You know better, Jimmy. The next time I catch you on the course looking for balls I'm going to call your parents. You boys get cracking; those leeches are sucking your blood."

Roger stumbled to the shore and handed his bag of balls to John, Jimmy had already given up his bag. John laughed as Jimmy and Roger scrambled to retrieve their clothes. He was sure they wouldn't venture back into the pond.

John called them leeches, but the kids called them bloodsuckers. Jimmy shook when he heard John say, "Those leeches are sucking your blood." He had a bloodsucker on his leg last summer; it hurt when he removed it. There must be thirty bloodsuckers on his legs now, and there were several on his stomach. Roger had bloodsuckers over his entire body. They moved quickly to get their clothes and walked home in their swimming trunks.

Jimmy's mother took the hose and rinsed their bodies. Than she sprinkled salt on the bloodsuckers while the boys lay on the grass. One by one the creatures fell off and she applied iodine with a cotton swab. The salt and the iodine stung, but the two culprits didn't complain. Jimmy's mother left them sitting in lawn chairs and went into the house to call the doctor.

Roger said to Jimmy, "We must have had fifty balls before John caught us. That was really hard giving him the golf balls."

"My legs started to feel funny right after we started; we should have believed the sign and gone fishing."

"It was fun going along the bottom and finding balls. If I had one of those special suits I would go back at night. You could find balls in the dark, you're under the water."

"I'll bet those suits cost a lot of money."

"The man that gets the balls goes to all the courses around here with that special suit. These bites don't hurt, but they itch like crazy. They're like mosquito bites."

Jimmy's mother came out of the house. "The doctor said to take it easy and there'll be no swimming for three days. He also said you could get an infection if you scratch the bite marks. You can use calamine lotion on those bites before you go to bed."

This was a story Jimmy and Roger weren't going to share with their friends. Jimmy's mother didn't ask how and where they had acquired the bloodsuckers. Ten-year-old boys learn by exploring their universe. She was sure that they wouldn't repeat the experience.

CHAPTER ELEVEN

More Frogs

Jimmy's family was hungry for frog legs and Jimmy and his father spent Friday night trying to catch some. It was apparent that others had discovered there were frogs along the golf course. They were out for two hours and only had six frogs. They would make a good snack, but there weren't enough for dinner.

Jimmy mentioned the dilemma to Mr. Marohn, and he offered another way to catch frogs. "When I was a boy I used a bamboo pole, a short piece of line, and a piece of red flannel tied on just above the hook. Bullfrogs are like bulls; they jump at anything red." He laughed heartily, "Maybe that's why they're called bullfrogs. Row along the shore and if you see a frog dangle the red flannel six inches from his head. When the frog jumps, you've got him. Frogs eat insects; they like to jump for their dinner."

Jimmy replied, "I'll have to look on Long Lake, I've never seen a bullfrog on Union Lake."

"Union Lake is too cold and deep for frogs, they like lily pads, swamp grass and warm shallow water. Start along the golf course and work your way around Long Lake. I did that twenty years ago and found plenty of frogs."

Jimmy and Roger were swimming in Long Lake. At the far end of the lake, there weren't any cottages and the shoreline was covered with swamp grass. Jimmy and his brother would paddle the canoe to the other side and turn around and come back. They were only interested in speed and how long it took them to get there and back. They didn't venture from the canoe to explore the shore.

Jimmy told Roger, "Mr. Marohn said you can catch frogs with a bamboo pole and a piece of red flannel. Let's take the canoe and look for frogs tomorrow."

"My family doesn't like frog legs, but it sounds like fun."

"We don't have to get up early, we're not going fishing. Let's start about nine."

"You'd better leave King in the garage; he'll get excited and tip the canoe over."

"You're right; he'd probably scare the frogs."

The next morning they put the canoe in the water and headed for the south shore. Jimmy had rigged a bamboo pole with a short line, a medium-sized hook and a piece of red flannel just above the hook. They started along the golf course and had gone a short distance when Roger spotted a frog. "I want to catch the first one."

"Go ahead; Mr. Marohn said to dangle the flannel six inches from his head."

Roger carefully extended the pole and placed the line perfectly in front of the frog. Seconds later he jumped and they had their first frog. "Did you see that!" Roger exclaimed.

"I saw it and we'll need at least twenty for dinner." Jimmy placed the frog in a burlap bag he packed with ice and put the bag in a pail. "You're good with the pole, I'll paddle and you catch the frogs. If we can find them it looks easy."

"It's better than catching fish; you can't see the fish take the bait. This is going to be fun."

Jimmy paddled along the golf course, but the weeds and lily pads protected the frogs. At the end of the course, cottages lined the way to a treed area at the end of the lake. Jimmy said, "There are no frogs here, let's paddle over to those trees."

In minutes they reached a marshy bank with lily pads and cat tails. Roger had the pole and Jimmy spotted a frog. Seconds later they had their second frog. Roger was now catching frogs at a good clip. Jimmy had his eyes glued to the marshy bank searching for frogs and he paddled the canoe into a small canal. There was a "NO TREPASSING" sign posted on the opposite bank, but they had their backs to the sign looking for frogs.

They were so intent on catching frogs they didn't see an inlet and a dock to their right. Roger had caught another frog, when a voice came from the dock. "Put that frog back in the water. Don't the schools teach you kids to read, or are you just dumb?"

Jimmy turned and saw a woman with a double barrel shotgun standing on the dock. The gun was pointed at the canoe. "There's a 'NO TREPASSING' sign back at the lake." She was angry and Jimmy thought she was going to shoot.

Jimmy stuttered, "I-I-I--didn't---see a sign--ma'am. You can have the frog."

"This is private property and those frogs are my pets. I told the kids I kicked out last week to stay out and tell their friends to stay out. Maybe if I shoot a couple of you kids the word will get out?" She lowered the gun and fired a shot in the water twenty feet to the rear of the canoe.

Roger stared at Jimmy, his eyes wide. Jimmy was busy turning the canoe around and wanted Roger's help. "Help me paddle; we have to get out of here." Roger put the pole down and grabbed the paddle.

The woman fired a second shot in the water. "If you're not out of here by the time I reload, I'm going to shoot both of you."

Jimmy and Roger paddled with all their strength and the canoe responded. They didn't turn around to see what the woman was doing, but it didn't take long to find out. Another shot rang out and Jimmy could hear the buckshot hit the water behind the canoe. He was sure the next shot would be in his back. He paddled harder.

The woman waved to the canoe, shouting, "Boys will be boys, but not with my frogs!"

Minutes later they were back in the lake and stopped to catch their breath. Roger had wet his pants. "I didn't see any sign, did you see a sign?"

"I saw it on the way out, it was on the other bank."

"You better not tell the other kids I wet my pants." Roger took his pants off. "I'm going in the water to rinse out my trunks and pants"

"I'm not going to tell anyone, my heart is still racing. I've never been so scared, she was really mad."

Roger came out of the water and Jimmy helped him back into the canoe.

Jimmy was shaking his head, "I've learned my lesson! I wouldn't trespass if you paid me. First the bloodsuckers and today we're almost shot. The kids in the *Our Gang* movies don't get in this much trouble."

Roger replied, "No one is gonna believe us. Would you believe the other kids? Look at my hands, I'm still shaking.

She said the frog were her pets. How can a bunch of frogs be pets?"

"My mother feeds the birds and says the birds are her friends. Maybe that's how that lady feels about the frogs."

"I guess you're right, most everyone feeds the birds and you can't pet them."

Jimmy said, "Let's keep going around the lake, maybe we can catch more frogs."

Roger replied, "I've got to stop shaking so I can hold the pole. Why was she trying to kill us over a couple of frogs?"

"She was shooting in the water; I think she was trying to scare us."

"She scared me, all right. Why didn't we see the sign?"

"We were looking at the bank, the sign was behind us." Jimmy paddled toward a clump of trees on the north side of the lake. There was a small swampy area, ideal for frogs. The boys regained their enthusiasm after Roger caught the second frog. Jimmy was keeping count; they had twenty-two large bullfrogs, more than enough for dinner. Jimmy said, "Its time for lunch, let's head for home. After lunch, we can go to the store and split a candy bar. We'll flip a coin, heads it's an Almond Joy, tails it's a Mounds bar."

Roger responded, "I get to flip the coin, I know its going to be tails."

Jimmy and Roger didn't heed the woman's advice; they kept the incident to themselves. If their parents heard the story, they might put restrictions on them.

CHAPTER TWELVE

The Turtle's Back

It was the third week in August, with only two more weeks of summer left. Jimmy and Roger wanted to catch another pike and they had been shut out at the spot where Roger caught the pike on opening day. Mr. Marohn said to fish in deeper water, about ten feet from the drop-off. He also suggested they cut one of their old bamboo poles in half. The shorter poles would be easier to work with if they had to pull the lines with their hands. Jimmy's brother laughed when he heard their plan. "Everyone knows that you need a rod and reel to fish in deep water for bass and pike."

Jimmy also wanted to check on the turtle, he hadn't seen her since the car backfired. He left King in the garage; he didn't want the dog barking at the turtle.

It was a beautiful summer day, and the temperature would be in the eighties. Roger untied the boat and pushed off. Jimmy wanted to fish opposite the bluff where he thought the turtle laid her eggs. From there they had a good look at the turtle's favorite spot near the old willow tree. Jimmy rowed to the drop-off and then retreated ten feet into deeper water before Roger dropped the anchor. They had forty feet of line on each pole with a heavy sinker. Mr. Marohn suggested they fish about three feet from the bottom, and slowly raise and lower the bait to attract the fish. The boys both released their lines until the sinkers reached the bottom. Roger placed his pole in the boat and carefully pulled his line up. He baited his hook with a minnow and dropped the line in the water. When it reached bottom, he wound the line around the pole to get the right length. There was no need for a bobber; you could feel a big fish on the line. They repeated the process with Jimmy's pole, and after ten minutes they were ready for the big pike.

When Jimmy turned to look at the fishing site he spotted the big turtle coming up the bank. He leaned forward and tapped Roger on the shoulder. "The turtle is back, she's lying next to the willow tree."

Roger looked to his right and spotted the turtle. He murmured, "I never thought we see that turtle again. We better not talk or make or a fuss, we might spook her."

"We haven't caught a pike or a bass since opening day, and our talking doesn't seem to bother her. If I get a strike, the heck with the turtle, I want to catch the fish."

"So do I," replied Roger.

The turtle lay peacefully on the beach with head and feet tucked inside her shell. There was little traffic on the road and she rested for an hour or more. Jimmy and Roger changed their minnows many times over but with no success, the pike weren't biting. Around nine the turtle slowly came out of her shell and headed for the water. Jimmy and Roger were out of minnows and headed to the dock. Roger knew from the way Jimmy was acting that he wanted to catch the turtle. "If you wanna catch the turtle, let's do it tomorrow, we have baseball practice on Thursday."

"That's a deal; you owe me for the bloodsuckers. I'll pick you up at seven and we can wait in the bushes like we did last time. I'll bring the gloves and the wash tub. Wear you trunks so you can run fast, 'cause I'll need your help right away."

"I still think the turtle's going to bite one of us, and I hope it isn't me. That turtle is the King Kong of Union Lake."

"I'll hold her down until you get there with the tub. Her flippers aren't feet, and she doesn't move fast on land. She might weigh forty pounds, but I'm bigger and stronger. She's not going anywhere if I'm on her back."

"If she bites your hand and scratches your arms you won't be holding on, you'll be crying for help. I still say we should leave the turtle alone."

"Don't chicken out on me."

"You're not a chicken, Jimmy, if it's something dumb and you know better, but I'll be ready."

CHAPTER THIRTEEN

The Next Day

Jimmy had trouble going to sleep; he was contemplating his confrontation with the turtle. Roger was right, if she bit his finger off he would have to give up. Something else bothered him; the turtle he saw yesterday looked larger than the one he saw in June. Mr. Marohn said there could be more than one. There was one thing for certain, it was a big turtle.

He was up early and careful not to wake his family as he dressed. King whimpered when Jimmy left him in the garage, but he didn't bark. Roger was waiting on the steps as Jimmy approached. He was full of enthusiasm, saying, "I think we can catch the turtle, but you have to be careful. Ron said the turtle can't bite you if you grab the shell behind her head. He said you could lie on her back with your right hand behind her head and use your left hand to grab her left leg so she can't get to the water. Once I'm there, I'll go to the other side and we can lift her into the tub. I think it will work."

Jimmy thought about Ron's suggestions and they seemed to make sense. You couldn't bite someone if they were standing behind you and you can't move your leg if someone has a good grip on it. "Those are good ideas. Let's get started; we want to be there before the turtle."

The sun was shining brightly over the horizon, and it was going to be a warm day. As they were putting their gear in the boat, Jimmy gazed across the bay at the fishing site; there were no cars or other activity. Roger pushed off and they reached the bushes minutes later. The turtle wasn't there and Roger wanted to be on the water side of the bush so he could arrive sooner with the tub. Jimmy agreed and they settled down to wait for their catch. Jimmy was tired and he put his head on his chest to rest. Roger was also tired from getting up early two days in a row and he soon fell asleep. A fly buzzing near his ear woke Jimmy, and he wasn't sure where he was. As the sleep lifted, he looked up at the sun to see what time it was. He lowered his eyes toward the willow tree and saw the turtle snuggled in her shell at the water's edge. His heart began to race. Roger sat straight up when Jimmy tapped him on the shoulder, but he remained silent. Jimmy pointed to the turtle, and Roger grinned. They observed the turtle for ten minutes, and her head and feet remained tucked in the shell. Jimmy's heart was now pounding and he could feel a knot in his stomach. Roger poked Jimmy, "What are you waiting for, she's sound asleep."

It was time to launch their plan, but all Jimmy could picture was the turtle biting his finger off and scratching his arms, his courage waning. Stalling for time he said, "You can't be sure the turtle is sleeping."

Roger whispered in Jimmy's ear. "You're afraid of the turtle, you're chicken. Wait till the kids hear about this; you'll never live it down."

Jimmy blushed, took a deep breath, sprang to his feet and knocked Roger down as he charged toward the turtle. The collision with Roger knocked him off balance and he slowed to right himself. It was difficult to run on the water's edge and his sneakers were spinning in the loose gravel as he lowered his head to regain his momentum. His legs felt heavy and it seemed liked he was taking forever to reach the turtle. *Why can't I go faster?* he wondered.

He had traveled half the distance before the turtle started toward the water. The rear legs and front flippers were kicking up sand and gravel. He picked up the pace and now he was twenty feet away and quickly closing the gap. Without warning his foot slipped on the loose gravel as he neared the turtle. He fought to keep his balance, but fell face forward with his arms extended, and slid on his chest into the turtle. It was a perfect slide to steal second base, but it wasn't part of the plan. He was partly in the water when his left hand and arm struck the turtle's rear right leg. The first thing he felt were the sharp claws that scratched at his glove and wrist as the turtle fought to get away. Jimmy braced himself with his left hand and grabbed the front of the shell with his right hand. He could feel the wrinkles in the turtle's neck as he secured his grip, and the turtle stretched her neck to bite him. His weight caused the turtle to lose momentum and she responded by scratching his left arm with her rear leg. Jimmy tried desperately to grab the turtle's leg to stop the punishment to his arm. Try as he may, he couldn't grasp the leg lying on his stomach with his right arm extended. Jimmy mumbled, "I need help. Where is Roger?"

Jimmy had knocked Roger down when he rounded the bush and the tub rolled into the water. Roger went after the tub and dropped it as he started to run. He picked up the tub a second time and headed toward Jimmy. He could see the turtle stretch her neck to bite him. The tub was big, he was small, and running with the tub was difficult. He lost his balance when he tried to run faster and joined his friend on the ground.

The turtle sensed she was winning the battle and tore at his arm with her sharp claws. The turtle was in the water and he could feel the power she was generating with her front flippers and rear legs.

Face down in the water, Jimmy was no match for the turtle, and there was no way he could hang on to the shell and right himself to climb on her back. His pulling on the shell with his right hand was turning the turtle toward him and he felt the tip of her nose brush his shoulder. His worst fears were being realized and reluctantly he let go of the shell before the turtle made another attempt to bite his shoulder. The splash from her churning flippers hit his face as she entered the shallow water and swam toward the safety of the drop-off. Jimmy pulled himself to his knees as the turtle disappeared from sight. He pounded the water with his fist to vent his frustration. He got to his feet and looked at his left arm and knees, seeing they were scratched and bleeding. *If I hadn't slipped on the gravel, I could have jumped on her back,* he thought.

Roger was out of breath when he reached Jimmy. "Let me see your shoulder, I'll bet it really hurts."

"Her nose hit my shoulder, and I let go before she tried to bite me again."

"I was getting up and it looked like she bit you. You wouldn't fool with that turtle if you saw the size of her mouth. She would have got you if you held on."

"I could feel her neck stretching and I could see her nose. Her neck got longer and longer and staring at her head and into her mouth is really scary."

"We would have had her if we didn't fall. You knocked me down when you left and the tub rolled into the water. I dropped the tub when I picked it up and I couldn't run fast carrying the tub. When I tried to run faster I fell down.

Look at your arm; I told you the claws were sharp. You're no chicken, Jimmy; I'm sorry I teased you." Roger was talking so fast he ran out of breath.

Jimmy inspected his arms. His left arm was bleeding where the turtle had scratched him. His shirt was torn, and he had pieces of gravel embedded in his knees. He waded into the shallow water to wash the blood from his arm, and carefully removed the gravel from his knees. The deep scratches the turtle made on his left arm were starting to burn. He gave Roger a determined look. "Next year we'll be bigger and stronger and we'll catch her."

Roger told Jimmy, "We need a net like they used to catch King Kong. We can make a net out of old clothesline. If she's tangled in the net, she can't scratch or bite us."

"That's a good idea; we won't need a wash tub if the turtle's caught up in the net."

Roger started to laugh, saying, "You've got more guts than brains. I'll never forget you lying on your stomach and wrestling with that turtle. It was better than the movies."

Jimmy started to laugh too, thinking it was better than crying. He picked up his gloves and threw them in the washtub. He put his arm on his friend's shoulder and they

93

walked to the boat. They were two pals who'd had a summer adventure together, sure to become a legend.

Jimmy told the story to his mother as she cleansed the scratches and covered them with iodine. The iodine burned and his arm hurt, but she assured him it was necessary to prevent infection. She bandaged the left arm; there would be no swimming for a while.

At dinner that night, Jimmy's brother and father thought he was stretching the story, but it took something big to make those scratches. Like most of the other residents who had lived on or near the lake for years, they had never spotted the big turtle. Jimmy lived at Union Lake until 1954 when he entered the Army. Neither he nor any of his friends or neighbors saw the turtle there again.

CHAPTER FOURTEEN

Summer's End

It was Jimmy's turn to bat. The boys from Union Lake had combined their baseball team with boys from Cedar Island Lake, Oxbow Lake, Round Lake, Long Lake, and Cooley Lake. It took six lakes and three boys from Detroit to field a team with nine players. They ended up with twelve players, but they needed at least two pitchers to play a seven-inning game. This was the game they had been practicing for all summer when they challenged the boys from Westacres. The boys from Westacres went to Union Lake School, and they were good friends. There were, however, several differences. The Westacre boys had coaches, good bats, lots of balls, and they practiced three times a week on a well-maintained field. They also had uniforms, baseball shoes and played several games a season. The

Union Lake team had two bats, a couple of balls, no uniforms, and they practiced once or twice a month on a corner lot they used for a field. No one on the Union Lake team had a pair of spikes (baseball shoes). They were fortunate a boy from Detroit had his own catcher's gear.

The players were ten to twelve years old. Oscar was almost thirteen and he was pitching for Westacres. He had a big curveball that made the hitters fall away from the plate. Union Lake was behind by nine runs and it was Jimmy's turn to bat. He had struck out twice and was determined to stay in the batter's box and hit the curve ball. It was the top of the seventh inning and there were two outs and two runners on base. Jimmy was staring at Oscar when he strode to the plate. He said to Oscar, "I can hit your curve ball."

"You're all talk. We'll see if you can hit my curve ball!"

The first two pitches were called strikes and Jimmy didn't take the bat off his shoulder. The next pitch was a high curve ball toward the outside of the plate and Jimmy hit it to right center field between the outfielders. He stood frozen at the plate admiring his hit. His teammates were urging him to run. The hit should have been an easy double, but the ball was in the fielder's glove when Jimmy slid into second base.

"You're out!" shouted the umpire.

Jimmy batted in two runs but made the last out at second base. His classmate Tom was playing second base. "Why didn't you run? That was an easy double."

"I couldn't believe I got a hit off Oscar. I just stood there and watched it; I forgot to run."

School was starting next week. Jerry and the other kids from Detroit would be leaving for the school year. Union Lake School only offered classes through the fifth grade; Jimmy and his classmates would be the oldest kids in school. The summer of 1943 was over, but the memories would live on.

DEDICATION

This book is dedicated to my sister-in-law Katherine.
She is a lover of books, an avid reader, and a sincere critic.

About the Book

The summer of 1943 is filled with adventure for two ten-year-old boys living at Union Lake. Jimmy spots a huge turtle basking in the sun at the fishing site, and he wants to catch it. He needs the assistance of his best friend, but Roger fears the ferocious bite of the turtle and the thought of losing a finger scares him. Finally Jimmy convinces him to help.

Jimmy and Roger are excited about the opening day of fishing season and Roger bets a quarter with his brother on how many fish they'll catch. He also wants Jimmy's help to hunt for balls at the golf course. Jimmy caddies at the course and he knows they aren't allowed to look for balls, but Roger won't take no for an answer. At summer's end, the boys are catching frogs and they get chased from a canal that is posted, "NO TRESPASSING."

JIMMY and the BIG TURTLE is a fun-filled romp with two boys who are discovering their universe.

PREVIEW

Was there ever a time when small boys were allowed to learn life's experiences by trial and error? A time when ten-year-old boys could fish, hunt for frogs, skip stones on the water, and dream of catching an enormous Leatherback Turtle by their own devices?

It's 1943 and this is the first summer Jimmy and Roger can use the boat on their own to fish for the really big bass and pike that are found in the cold, deep waters of Union Lake. While exploring the lake, Jimmy spots a huge Leatherback Turtle swimming on the bottom of the lake. When he describes the turtle to Mr. Marohn the shopkeeper, he learns that big Leatherback Turtles populated the lake when Marohn was a boy forty years ago. Jimmy is awestruck when he spots a big Leatherback Turtle basking in the sun at the fishing site. He determines that the turtle is two feet in diameter and from that moment on, he wants to catch it. His best friend Roger fears the ferocious bite of the turtle and the thought of losing a finger makes him reluctant to help. Jimmy won't take no for an answer, and convinces his friend that he needs him and Roger agrees.

As the boys plan for the opening day of fishing season, Jimmy relives an old experience when he hooked himself in the back of the head with his brother's casting rod. Undaunted, Jimmy and Roger buy their gear, dig for worms and catch minnows to use on opening day. A confident Roger bets a quarter with his older brother that they'll catch twenty-five fish. They come up short on the quantity but long on the size of the fish they catch.

Later in the summer Roger devises a plan to hunt for golf balls at the local golf course. Small boys aren't allowed on the course and the pond with the golf balls is marked with a sign reading, "DANGEROUS WATER," but that doesn't bother Roger. When they're caught by the course superintendent and come out of the water, they're covered with bloodsuckers.

The following week Mr. Marohn explains to Jimmy how he caught large frogs when he was a boy. Thus, following suit and using a bamboo pole and a piece of red flannel, Jimmy and Roger are so intent on catching frogs they paddle their canoe into a private canal on Long Lake. They quickly learn at the wrong end of a rifle that some people consider frogs to be pets.

At summer's end, they spot the big Leatherback Turtle basking in the sun at the fishing site. Finally, after Jimmy has spent two months in preparation for this day, the turtle has returned. As the boys hoped, the turtle again comes to the fishing site the next day and the two are waiting for her.

JIMMY and the BIG TURTLE takes place in an idyllic time when small boys were allowed to roam free from morning until night; and their greatest worries were how to catch the largest fish, and the largest turtle.

ABOUT THE AUTHOR

Jim Haskin lives in the State of Washington, is married, and has five daughters and thirteen grandchildren. He enjoys writing, golf, sailing, and the theatre. His home is located on Kelsey Creek in Bellevue, and Jim enjoys watching the returning salmon navigate the creek in the fall.

Often during discussions around the dinner table his children and grandchildren would ask, "What was it like when you were young? What went on during World War II, and how did it affect your life."

His three books, *Jimmy and the Big Turtle*, *Jimmy and the Secret Letter*, and *The War is Over* tell the story of life during the great war for two boys growing up in Union Lake, Michigan.

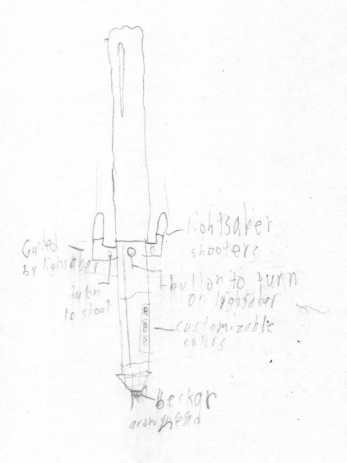

Guided by lightsaber

lightsaber shooters

button to shoot

+button to turn on lightsaber

customizable colors

beskar arrowhead

Made in United States
North Haven, CT
04 March 2022